School
Anarchy

(Bad, BAD Children)

Chris Greave

Text & Graphics
Copyright © 2017 Chris Greave

ISBN-13: 978-0995586802
ISBN-10: 0995586802

Lightship Guides & Publications

(lightshipguides@gmail.com)

I dreamily dozed;
Was 'bout eight in the morning,
My eyes were all sleepy and blurred,
The alarm on the dresser was buzzing,
To get up now was simply absurd.

I yawned as I thought of the morning:
Another day back at the grind;
The blankets were far better comfort,
To leave them - a thought quite unkind.

But leave them I must for school beckoned,
Like an evil thing warping my mind,
I'd much rather be watching tele
Than in that learning prison confined.

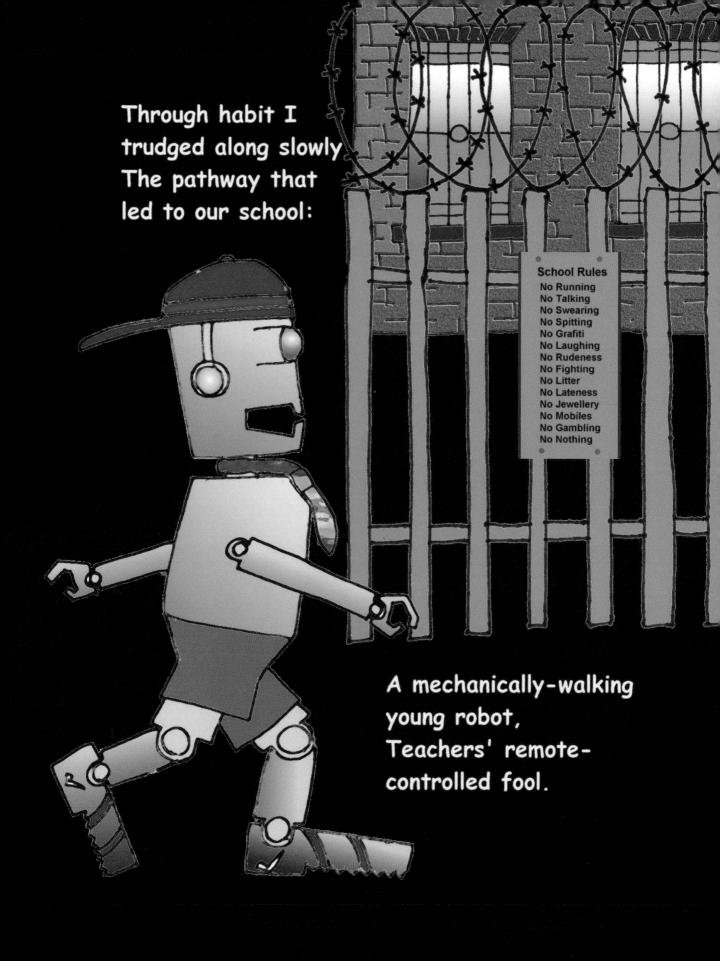

I arrived in my classroom just early
Enough not to be marked late,
The others were equally dismal,
Awaiting a similar fate.

It was this morbid situation
Which provoked me to question my lot:
"Avoid slavishly serving the teachers"
Was the quest of this following plot.

Now why should it be that we listen
Intently to what teachers say?
Let's see if a reversed situation
Can alter our sullen dismay.

So charged with this sparkling fervour
I endeavoured to further my cause:
Written on dingy rough paper,
I secretly passed round this verse:

"Dearest scholars and colleagues,
Say 'pooh' to the teachers' reign,
We'll start to rule in this building,
We'll make it our domain.
We'll smash the desks and the cupboards,
Plaster the ceiling with scrawls,
Let's write all over the blackboard,
And paint all over the walls.

"Swipe chalk, rulers and pencils,
Dismantle the cloakroom hooks,
And in the 'respectable' library
Pour ink all over the books;

But in the science laboratory
We'll preserve all that we find
– How else can the art of explosions
And bomb-making be refined?

"And so dearest scholars and colleagues
This vision to you I address;
Let's convert this place of learning
Into a mind-splitting terrible mess."

So we all trooped
   off to assembly
Where Headmaster was
   preaching his spiel.
Then the deadly hush
   of the hallroom
Was split by an
   echoing squeal:
Headmistress was
   clasping her bottom,
Some gum had stuck
   to her dress;
The shot of some
   pea-shooting villain,
(A remarkable aim,
   I confess.)

She sat down, for the shock made her tremble,
Alas, she sat down without care,
For the chewing gum stuck to her bottom
Cemented her firm to the chair.

Us pupils buckled with laughter,
Headmaster ranted with rage,
Picked up his lectern to hush us
By stamping it hard on the stage.
Alas, that also got splintered,
It buckled completely in two;
But then he was
   writhing in agony –
The lectern had crashed
      on his shoe.

The teachers dismissed us hurriedly,
We raced out cheering with joy,
And sped to our first lesson's venue
To plan for our next ploy.

Rude things on the blackboard were written
Displaying our moral decline:
Embarrassing tales about teachers,
Unmentionable in this little rhyme.

The door was open just slightly
We placed a pile of books overhead;
As our teacher entered the classroom
The crash made him fall almost dead!

So, in the history classroom
We scattered pins
   on teacher's chair,
As the history teacher
   descended:
Ahhhh! She shot up
   ten foot in the air.

The caretaker, that dawdling old doddle,
Decided to disappear,
Locked himself away in the storeroom
Where he couldn't stop shaking with fear.

The sports teacher, strong-muscled and burly
Challenged the pupils' revolt;
Though he thought he was Wonderwoman
His bionics suffered a jolt;

For climbing gymnasium wallbars,
And swinging like apes on the ropes,
Screaming school kids pounced on the teacher,
Negating his bionic hopes.

In the school garden compound,
Where roses blushed with pride,
We helpfully filled the watering can
From the jar labelled "Cyanide".
Prize roses, petunias and dahlias
Were sprayed as the watering can tilted;

As the botany teacher approached us,
The blooming geraniums wilted.
The teacher, concerned at the puzzle,
Was shocked at this stage of ado;
As the pansies around him were fading,
He felt a prize pansy too!

With our trays held at the ready
We hurriedly shoved in the queue,
Filled our own plates with sizable helpings
Of beans, chips and ...Irish stew!

The smash was flicked round the canteen,
The peas marbled over the floor,
Potatoes made excellent missiles,
And gravy got smeared on the door.

Eyefuls of custard and treacle
Hit teachers who'd entered the fray;
On the floors which were covered in omelettes
The teachers fled 'scrambling' away!

A truce was called after dinner,
A meeting was held by the staff;
So to pry on the proceedings
We viewed through the window to laugh.

A hundred laughing child faces
Were squashed 'gainst the window pane,
Like a plague of inescapable vultures
We drove the teachers completely insane.

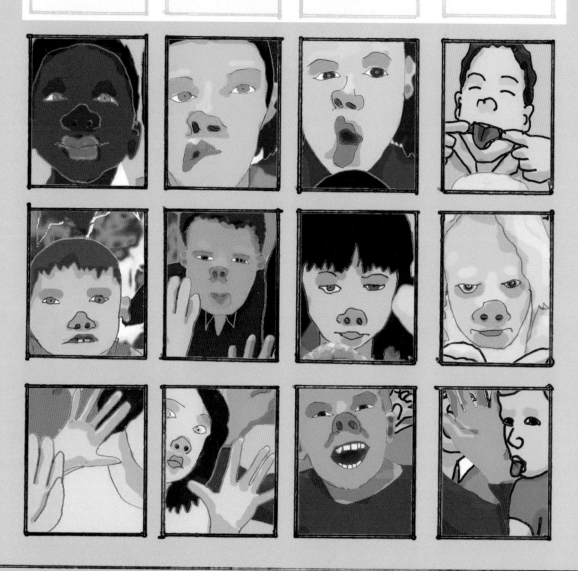

Like a swarm of ravishing locusts
We stormed through the window pane;
The teachers fled like scared cowards,
AND WERE NEVER SEEN AGAIN!

Now, from the tale as I so far have told it
Utopia was here - it would seem;
But, back to school for you who don't listen,
For I said it was only a dream.

So I awoke, was gone eight in the morning,
My eyes were still sleepy and blurred,
The alarm on the dresser still buzzing,
Reveille at last had occurred.

Now the moral of this little fable
Is that dreams seldom come true;
But of course, there's no harm in trying:
It'll teach the teachers a lesson or two.

Printed in Great Britain
by Amazon